A-U-T-I-S-T-I-C?

How Silly Is That!

I don't need any labels at all

Lynda Farrington Wilson

A-U-T-I-S-T-I-C? How Silly Is That!

All marketing and publishing rights guaranteed to and reserved by:

FUTURE HORIZONS INC.

721 W. Abram Street
Arlington, TX 76013
(800) 489-0727
(817) 277-0727
(817) 277-2270 (fax)
E-mail: *info@fhautism.com*
www.fhautism.com

ISBN 9781935274599

"This sweet and endearing book offers youngsters a fresh perspective on autism, by helping them understand that autism is just one small facet of who they are!"

– Rebecca Moyes, MEd, author of *Visual Techniques for Developing Social Skills* and *Building Sensory Friendly Classrooms* and mother of a young man with Asperger's syndrome

Dedication

To all of our children who may have been seen by their label, and not for their brilliance of heart, mind, and spirit...by God's grace, may they continue to shine, shine, shine!

To M.H. and all of the teachers, therapists, and family members who support a child with special needs, but who never considered how silly a label really is...teach this lesson to all who will listen with the same love, passion, and dedication you give to our children.

To my family, who have always seen Tyler's gifts, embraced his difference of mind, and encouraged and inspired me when I needed it most.

And to Tyler...for giving us all the gift of tiny miracles, each and every day.

Or if being left handed makes me...

I can swim like a fish so I guess that would make me...

If I catch a fish, am I **FISHER-TISTIC?**

And if I cook the fish, would that make me **CULINARI-TISTIC,** too?

I love to eat donuts and jelly beans and ice cream. Does that make me

JUNK-FOOD-TiSTiC or

SUGAR-CRAVIN'-TiSTiC

or just plain...

yum!

LOVES-DONUTS-JELLY-BEANS-AND-iCE-CREAM-TiSTiC?

I am really good in math,
which I think would make me

MATH-TISTIC,

but I'm not so good
in history, so would I also be

HISTOR-ISTIC or, quite possibly,

NON-HISTOR-ISTIC?

My feet are sort of big,
and my teeth are not straight.
So would I be considered

BiG-FOOT-ORTHODONT-iSTiC?

Hysterical!

I have autism. A part of me feels overloaded some of the time, and social situations are awkward. And well, communicating is a bit of a challenge because my brain is just wired in its own way.

uh, hi.

Does that make me
BROWN-HAIR-TISTIC,
SOUTH-PAW-TISTIC,
AQUA-TISTIC, FISHER-TISTIC,
CULINARI-TISTIC,
JUNK-FOOD-TISTIC,
SUGAR-CRAVIN'-TISTIC,
LOVES-DONUTS-JELLY-BEANS-ICE-CREAM-TISTIC,
MATH-TISTIC, HISTOR-ISTIC,
BIG-FOOT-ORTHODONT-ISTIC
AND **AUTISTIC?**

15

WHEW! Ridiculous! I don't need any labels at all. I'm just a typical person, with my own likes and dislikes, strengths and weaknesses, hopes and dreams, who approaches the world a little differently...but many times, better.

I'm a brilliant person WITH autism.

A-U-T-I-S-T-I-C?
How Silly Is That!

I rock!

Author's Note

The incidence of autism has grown exponentially in the past decade, bringing new challenges in how to educate, integrate, and approach a child with autism. I have sat in many an IEP meeting where my son, Tyler, was referred to as *autistic*—not as a good student, a Boy Scout, a violin player, or a sweet and caring young man, but just *autistic*. In contrast, when I suggested that my son spend time in his school's sensory room, a teacher told me she didn't want him to be around those "autistic kids" because it might set him back (in this case, those "autistic kids" she was referring to were children on the lower-functioning end of the autism spectrum, as compared to Tyler). How sad on both accounts—that our children are referred to by their disability first and as people second.

Some may find my viewpoint debatable, as there are many people on the autism spectrum that find identity, inclusion, or even solace in the label of *autistic,* and I respect that. I, too, can introduce myself as an author, artist, mother, or gardener, which is *my choice* of an identity on any given day or situation. However, when *we* label our children, especially in a way that can negate all their other gifts and talents, we've altered society's perception of that child, and, with that, we may even be prohibiting their academic and social advancement.

With advocacy, our society as a whole has become "socially corrected" on many labels used for ethnic groups, disabilities, and the like. The guidelines of the American Medical Association style manual and that of the American Psychological Association suggest that we avoid language that objectifies a person by his or her condition (eg, "autistic"). They advise that we use "people-first" language, instead of focusing on an individual's disability or chronic condition (such as substituting the phrase, "with autism").

The book you hold in your hands is my advocacy, to help the world see the exceptional brilliance in our children *with autism.* There isn't a day that goes by that I am not in awe of my son Tyler's mind and how he approaches the world in a way unlike mine, but better in so many ways. I've often thought that perhaps the pureness of mind and spirit that people on the autism spectrum bring to us may be an evolution that is meant to heal our broken world and even our hearts. I pray each day that I am worthy of Tyler and the hard, hard challenges he works to overcome. I am mindful that his success will be built upon opportunity, not a restrictive label that may bring fear, prejudice, and alienation. I hope you enjoy *A-U-T-I-S-T-I-C? How Silly Is That!,* my poignant yet lighthearted approach to educating people of all ages about how autism is just a small part of a whole person.

18

~Lynda Farrington Wilson

About the Author

Lynda Farrington Wilson is an artist and former marketing executive, whose talents and experiences have culminated in writing, illustrating, and advocating for children with autism and Sensory Processing Disorder. Lynda and her husband live in North Carolina and have two beautiful daughters-in-law and three wonderful sons, the youngest of whom is a funny, brilliant, and talented sensory seeker who has autism.

Her first book, *Squirmy Wormy, How I Learned to Help Myself*, was endorsed by Temple Grandin. *Squirmy Wormy* helps children understand their sensory issues while providing easy, everyday activities for self-regulation. When she's not advocating, Lynda works from home as an illustrator and can occasionally be found "playing in the mud" on her potter's wheel.

www.lyndafarringtonwilson.com

Another great title by Lynda!

"*Squirmy Wormy* is a cute and funny picture book that will help elementary school children understand sensory problems."
— Temple Grandin, PhD

Other Children's Books

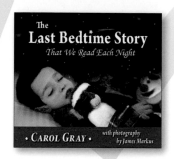

All of these titles and more are at www.FHautism.com

Additional Resources

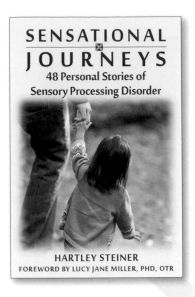

SENSATIONAL JOURNEYS
48 Personal Stories of Sensory Processing Disorder

HARTLEY STEINER
FOREWORD BY LUCY JANE MILLER, PHD, OTR

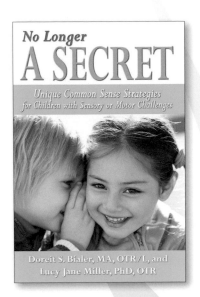

No Longer **A SECRET**

Unique Common Sense Strategies for Children with Sensory or Motor Challenges

Doreit S. Bialer, MA, OTR/L, and Lucy Jane Miller, PhD, OTR

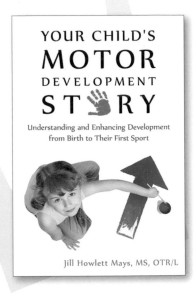

YOUR CHILD'S MOTOR DEVELOPMENT STORY

Understanding and Enhancing Development from Birth to Their First Sport

Jill Howlett Mays, MS, OTR/L

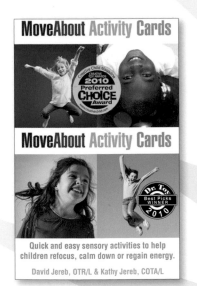

MoveAbout Activity Cards

MoveAbout Activity Cards

Quick and easy sensory activities to help children refocus, calm down or regain energy.

David Jereb, OTR/L & Kathy Jereb, COTA/L

Building Sensory Friendly Classrooms

to support children with challenging behaviors

"Lots of practical information that teachers can use to help children with sensory problems. I wish my teachers had had this book when I was a child."

— Dr. Temple Grandin, author of *The Way I See It and Thinking in Pictures*

REBECCA MOYES

Implementing Data Driven Strategies!

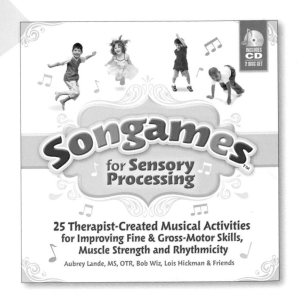

Songames for Sensory Processing

25 Therapist-Created Musical Activities for Improving Fine & Gross-Motor Skills, Muscle Strength and Rhythmicity

Aubrey Lande, MS, OTR, Bob Wiz, Lois Hickman & Friends

BEHAVIOR SOLUTIONS for the Inclusive Classroom

A Must-Have for Teachers!

See a Behavior

BETH AUNE, OTR/L
BETH BURT & PETER GEN...

MORE BEHAVIOR SOLUTIONS IN and BEYOND the Inclusive Classroom

Companion to the Bestseller!

A Must-Have for Teachers and Other Educational Professionals!

BETH AUN...
BETH B...
PETER GE...

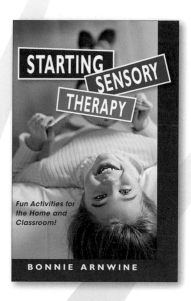

STARTING SENSORY THERAPY

Fun Activities for the Home and Classroom!

BONNIE ARNWINE

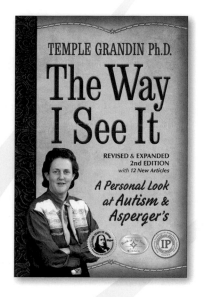

TEMPLE GRANDIN Ph.D.

The Way I See It

REVISED & EXPANDED 2nd EDITION with 12 New Articles

A Personal Look at Autism & Asperger's

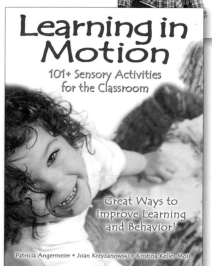

Learning in Motion

101+ Sensory Activities for the Classroom

Great Ways to Improve Learning and Behavior!

Patricia Angermeier • Joan Krzyzanowski • Kristina Keller Moir

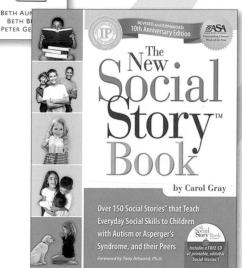

REVISED and EXPANDED 10th Anniversary Edition

The New Social Story Book

by Carol Gray

Over 150 Social Stories™ that Teach Everyday Social Skills to Children with Autism or Asperger's Syndrome, and their Peers

Includes a FREE CD of printable, editable Social Stories!

Foreword by Tony Attwood, Ph.D.

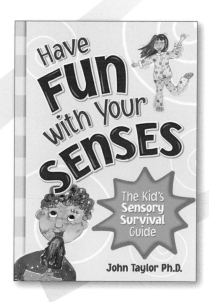

Have Fun with your SENSES

The Kid's Sensory Survival Guide

John Taylor Ph.D.

Find these and other great resources at www.FHautism.com

These catalog companies can provide more ideas and products for kids with special needs.

School Specialty
(888) 388-3224
www.schoolspecialtyonline.net

FlagHouse Sensory Solution
(800) 793-7900
www.FlagHouse.com

Henry Occupational Therapy Services, Inc.
(623) 882-8812
www.ateachabout.com

Therapro, Inc.
(800) 257-5376
www.theraproducts.com